Never
Lose Hope

DESTINEE A. DelBONIS

NEVER LOSE HOPE

ONE

I DON'T KNOW WHAT HURT MORE, MY BODY OR MY
heart. I was staring at his ceiling through one blood-shot eye as screams faded in and out of my ears.

"You bit...are...kidding me?" His voice cut through me like a knife through butter.

Tears ran down my cheeks as the yelling got louder, clearer.

"Don't be such a cry...you little bi—"

Now I could only hear the sound of my name.

"Hope! Hope! Hope!"

I twisted away from the noise and my breath shortened. I was being shaken.

"*Hope!*"

"No! No! No! No!" I retaliated as I squirmed away.

It was a different voice now. A female voice.

"Hope! Hope Rae Abuso, get your ass out of bed.

1

We have American Lit in *fifteen minutes*," She was shaking me back and forth.

My eyes shot open to find a pair of bright blue eyes over me with a half-empty bottle of Tito's in her hand.

"What is *this?*" she snapped.

It took me a moment to calm myself down and feel the floor beneath me. I looked to my right and saw a cork next to me, along with a few shot glasses and my phone. 7:19. *Crap.*

I sat up and ran my hands over my face and through my hair. "Got carried away last night, Carmen," I mumbled groggily.

"Whatever." She rolled her eyes. She was used to this behavior from me by now. "You had the same dream again," she said in a more sympathetic tone. "I could tell."

I was silent. She went on, this time in a whisper, as if there were more people in our dorm. "Have you talked to him?"

"Yeah... let's get going," I answered a little too quickly.

I threw my hair in a messy knot, found a pair of sweats that I had worn twice this week already, and followed Carmen out the door. She was babbling about last night with her ex but I was still either too hungover or too shaken up (probably a little of both) to pay attention. I threw my books on my desk and put my head down as Carmen sat down next to me and batted her long eyelashes at some boy sitting across the room.

My phone vibrated and I opened my eyes. *You didn't say good morning to me. Again.* I sighed heavily and threw it in my bag just as Mr. Don trudged in with a stack of papers. He was a short guy, but his personality made him seem oddly tall. His scruff was the color of tar and his tired eyes were a deep brown. He scanned the room before giving us his infamous Monday morning lecture.

"Mid-term papers. I graded them, to put it lightly." He slammed the pile on his desk. "They sucked."

He glugged his coffee and continued. "You guys seriously gotta step it up. I don't know if you all have been partying too much or you're having *problems* in your relationships, but I didn't want to spend my weekend grading half-ass essays on the Boston Tea Party."

My blood went cold. I could feel the vodka in my stomach bubbling up.

"Mr. Don, may I go to the bathroom?" I dashed out of the room before I could even hear his answer.

I grabbed the wall as I quickly limped down the hallway. It was oddly quiet. I leaned my back against it, shut my eyes, and took a deep breath. Inhale, exhale. Inhale, exhale. Inhale...

Bang. The next thing I knew, I was being dragged into the girl's lavatory. Two large, callused hands had my wrists pinned against the wall and a pair of feet crushed my tiny toes. My bag fell to the floor and all of the contents spilled out.

"You think you can just ignore me, bitch? Huh?" His breath tickled my neck and went right down my spine as I started to scream. His hand slammed against my face and I keeled over in pain, unable to get any noise or word out. His arms had my wrists so tight in his hands that they were turning red.

"Answer my goddamn question. I'm not gonna ask you again." He kicked my leg and raised his fist for a second time.

"No, no, no, I'm sorry! I'm sorry," I wailed. "I'm sorry."

He frantically looked around the room. "Alright. Alright, just relax." He let go of his grip and I fell to the floor. His condescending eyes stared me down and he helped me up.

"Hey," he said softly as he turned my chin to his face. "I love you." His lips pressed against mine and I melted. He stomped out of the bathroom and I turned to the mirror to look at the damage. Only red on the face and a bruise on my leg, not too bad. I took a deep breath as a silent tear fell down my cheek. Suddenly my mind took me back fifteen years.

My mother was in the bathroom, wearing far too much makeup and still applying more to her right eye.

"Mommy?" I whispered as I peeked through the door, holding my teddy bear.

"Oh, honey, hi." She whipped her head around and had a smile plastered on her face. Her face seemed happy, but her eyes were full of sadness.

"Mommy, why are you crying?" I asked.

She knelt down so we were face-to-face, and I could see that her left cheek was about double the size of her right.

"Was it Daddy again?" I said in a hush, and wiped her pouring tears.

"Yes, dear, it was." Her head fell for a moment and she looked back up at me with a tear-stricken face. "Hopie, promise me something."

"Okay." I smiled, my adolescent self confused as to what was happening.

"Don't you ever, and I mean, ever, let a man lay a finger on you. Because if they do, they are a sorry excuse for a man. Promise me that, honey."

"Okay, Mommy." I paused. "But, if Daddy does that to you, then why do you still love Daddy?"

Mom became hysterical and held me tight to her chest.

I looked up at the ceiling for a moment, and shook my head. "I'm fine," I said to reassure myself. "I'm fine."

"No you're not," said a voice behind me.

I spun around and saw a little Asian girl staring at

me, her eyes wide as saucers. She coughed for a few seconds and continued.

"I was in that stall." She pointed as she tentatively stepped towards me. "Are you okay?"

"Yeah...yeah, I'm fine," I replied as I searched for my compact on the floor and started applying powder to my face. I continued this as we stood in silence until I dropped the makeup to the ground and realized that I was exactly like my mother. I stared back up at the ceiling and barely whispered, "I'm sorry."

"Huh?" said the girl.

"It's nothing, it's just..." My mind was racing. I couldn't stop shaking. "It's just that...well, I mean..."

I burst into tears and ran into the arms of a girl I did not know. She tightly embraced me in return, and whispered, "Shh, it's okay. You're going to be okay. It's over."

"No," I sniffled, "it's not." I shakily sighed and appreciated her comfort as we stood there in silence.

After what seemed like a while she looked at me with concern and said, "Um, I hate to ask you this, but, if he did that to you, then why do you still love him?"

TWO

I STOOD THERE, FROZEN. THE GIRL SENSED MY uncertainness and continued. "Sorry. I'm Astrid." She began to pick up my stuff. "I just transferred here from Ohio." I noticed her English was slightly broken.

I joined her on the floor and broke the tension. "Wow," I said awkwardly, "so, have you always lived in Ohio or—"

"No, no. I was born in Korea but we had to leave when I was just a little girl." She turned away. "Dad and Mom died in a car crash, had to move in with *Halmeoni*." Her gaze matched mine and she chuckled. "It means 'Grandma.'"

"That must have been really hard for you," I replied, and took her hand as we both stood up. "You're so brave."

"I guess," she answered modestly. "But, back to you. Does that," she motioned to my cheek, "always happen?"

"It's not that bad this time. I've seen worse. My dad did the same thing to my mom, but he's locked up somewhere in Cleveland."

For a moment, I could see a tear well up in her eye. She sniffled and replied, "Listen, I'm not trying to tell you what to do or anything, but I think you need to end things with him." She looked at me thoughtfully. "You're not happy. I can see it in your eyes."

Astrid dashed out of the bathroom and I stood there, dumbfounded. My mind was spinning, my face was hurting, and my heart was broken. I gathered the rest of my things and walked out the door. Second period bell was about to ring. I took out my phone to see it spammed with messages from Carmen: *Girl, where are you? Mr. Don is BORING af. Omg!! James keeps looking at me! H?*

I rolled my eyes and answered, *Had a hair emergency. Met a friend, too.*

I scanned the hallway before uneasily walking to my locker. I grabbed my books and my phone buzzed yet again, but this time not from Carmen. *One new friend request: AstridYin27.*

Accept. I smiled to myself just as the bell rang. I began to walk to Calculus but not before I was stopped by Jonah, a garrulous blonde athlete who I had a few other classes with.

"Hey, Hope!" he exclaimed as he opened his locker. "You'll never believe what just happened.

Carmen was talking to James and—" He abruptly stopped and took a step towards me. His hand grazed my cheek and softly but sternly murmured, "It was him again, wasn't it?"

I backed up and pulled out my water bottle, drank it for far too long, and answered, "It's not a big deal. It was all a misunderstanding." I took another sip and cringed.

"He did this to you."

Sip.

"When did this happen?"

Sip. Cringe.

"Hope, you've got to listen to me. You *can't* keep doing this to yourself. You're worth so much more than this."

Three sips.

Jonah snatched the bottle out of my hands and threw it in the trash can fifteen feet away, a perfect three-pointer. "If you think you can just go through life putting vodka in your water bottles and acting like you're happy in your relationship, you're dead wrong." He slammed his locker shut and stormed off down the hallway. But before he turned the corner he stopped. He whirled around and stomped back in my direction. When he reached me, our faces were so close that I could smell the coffee and gum on his breath.

"You need to talk to your dad about this," Jonah whispered. He slowly backed away and I did not breathe until I watched him turn that corner.

THREE

THE DAY PASSED RATHER QUICKLY AND BY THE TIME
I got back to the dorm, Carmen had left me a note on
my dresser: *Studying at James's dorm (wink, wink). I'll
spill later! Xo, —C*

I was so glad to be home alone. I walked into the
bathroom and stared myself down in the mirror. I
went to touch my face but my ears started ringing
from the pain. I took off my sweats to find a bruise
the size of a baseball on my left leg. A painful sob
escaped my body and I went in the shower. I tried
washing my leg but I wailed out in pain the second
the soap seeped into my skin. I couldn't hold back the
tears anymore. I fell to the shower floor and sobbed
uncontrollably, for minutes, hours, I don't really
know. I shook violently, screaming in pain and frustration, dizzy from my thoughts. I gasped for air and

kept telling myself not to cry, not to be weak.

"Hope?" a voice said nervously.

I screamed, turned the shower head off, and peeked my head out, my body wrapped in the shower curtain.

Carmen and Astrid were standing there, both looking very concerned.

"We're really sorry," Carmen said as she stepped forward.

"I could hear you from my dorm down the hall," said Astrid. "I called Carmen and we both talked. We agree that this has to stop."

"Honey, come here." Carmen had a towel open for me and I wrapped myself in it as she examined my leg.

"Jesus," she whispered. "This is worse than the last time." Carmen ran out of the bathroom and to the kitchen where we kept ice, bandages, and Advil— the usual.

Astrid knelt beside me. "Hope, there's something I need to tell you. I—"

Carmen rushed into the bathroom, her arms empty. But what followed her was another person.

"Jonah?" I nearly yelled, both embarrassed and confused as to why he was here. I jumped behind Astrid.

"Sorry, uh, nice towel." He smirked. I pulled it tight to my chest as I squirmed awkwardly to cover myself. I shot a glare at Carmen, but she looked quite content.

My eyes darted from him to Carmen, to Astrid, to him, back to Carmen, and back to him.

"I just, um, I came to bring you these." He sheepishly stepped forward and helped me up, and reached in his back pocket to pull out two sheets of paper.

"Plane tickets," he said. "So you can go see your dad."

I looked at him in disbelief. I opened my mouth to speak just as Carmen cut me off. "Aw, isn't that the sweetest thing? He bought tickets for you and me to go to Ohio," she said as she linked her arm in mine, my towel slipping by the second.

"Oh, well, I kind of actually—" Jonah began.

Now Astrid butted in. "Actually, Carmen, I think that if she were to go to Ohio, she should go with *me,* considering that I lived there and I actually know what I'm doing." She coughed again for a solid minute.

Carmen fired back. "I'm sorry, but *who's* her best friend?"

"Guys, just chill out!" Jonah groaned.

"Who made you the peacemaker?" Astrid snapped.

"Everyone just calm down!" I hollered, and the room fell silent. *Buzz. Buzz.* My phone was vibrating next to the sink and the four of us exchanged looks and lunged to grab it. Carmen and Astrid played tug of war with it until Carmen snatched it from her hands, leaving Jonah and me tangled up while I was in a pink fuzzy towel.

"Well, she's not here right now," Carmen said, her eyes darting around the room. "She's...making up a few assignments at school...yeah, well I don't think she will be in the mood to speak to *you* anyway... what? I already told you she's not here! Hello?" She slammed the phone on the counter.

Fear filled her voice and her eyes. "He said he's right down the hall. Guess my story wasn't very convincing," she told us.

"I'm gonna go," coughed Astrid, and she ran out of the dorm like her life depended on it.

Jonah and I were still in the same position that we were before, our eyes locked. "He's not gonna touch you," a stern Jonah told me.

"No, but he will hurt *you* if he finds out there's another guy in this room that's not him," I whispered faintly.

Knock. Knock. Knock. We all froze and turned our heads to the door. Carmen's voice startled me when she hushed, "Listen, I can stall him. You two need to hide. *Now.*"

"The closet!" I exclaimed. I hugged my towel to my chest, grabbed Jonah's arm and led him into the tiny space, barely able to squeeze the both of us. It was dark and crammed, and our noses practically touched. We were both breathing heavily and quickly.

"Let me go out there," Jonah said. "I can show this bastard what's up."

"No," I barked, "You are *not* going out there with him. Carmen is fine, she can handle herself."

"Are you saying I can't?"

"No, well, I mean I just don't want you to—" I paused. "You haven't been around him."

"Oh, yes, because you can handle yourself perfectly fine around him, right?"

"How dare you say that to me!"

"Why not? Look at you!"

Our breathing was getting faster by the second. We stood there quiet, staring at each other, only communicating with our looks.

Meanwhile, Carmen swung open the door and forced a smile as she squeaked, "Oh, hi! How nice to see you!"

"Cut the crap, Carmen. I know she's here." he said threateningly.

"Actually, she just ran out to the All-Nighter to grab some...milk. Said she'd be there a while."

"You said on the phone that she was making up classwork."

"Oh...yeah, well...she *was*, but then she left."

"Well, I guess I'll just have to wait here for her until she comes back." He shoved Carmen to the side and took a seat on my bed, his hands gripping the sheets and his leg bouncing a mile a minute.

Carmen frantically looked for an excuse to get him out. "I'm not sure you want to stay. I have a date tonight. Here. And I think I'm going to make it *the night*, if you know what I mean." She winked.

"Well, I'm sure you can find other arrangements," he growled. "Perhaps a sketchy alley?"

Carmen whipped out her phone and desperately moved her thumbs around.

My phone buzzed. *Loudly.*

FOUR

"WILL YOU SHUT THAT DAMN THING OFF?" HE mouthed.

Not budging. SOS!

I turned the screen to Jonah's face and he started to shake. I grabbed his arm and we stood there for a minute or two.

"Um," I whispered as I released my hand, "what do we do?"

This time, he reached for my hand. "Whatever happens, I swear, he won't lay a finger on you."

"What was that?" He gazed around the room.

Carmen smiled anxiously, gripping her phone tightly. "She said she's going to your dorm. Might wanna check there."

"Bullshit," he yelled, and snagged her phone right out of her hands. "I'm not an idiot. Show me where the bitch is."

"Not happening."

He shot up and grabbed her arms so tightly that he could lift her in the air. "I'm gonna ask you one last time, hoe. *Tell me where she is.*"

Carmen broke out sobbing, "No! You're not going to touch her."

"Maybe I should touch you then," he breathed, and pressed a hard kiss on her neck.

"Touch either of them, and you're going six feet under." The closet door opened and Jonah stormed out, my hand still in his, both of us refusing to let go.

"Who the hell are you?" He hollered, dropping Carmen to the floor. He turned to me. "What the hell were you doing in that closet with him, you slut?" He began to march towards me, his whole body enraged, just as Jonah put a fist to his jaw. He fired back with a punch straight to his nose, but Jonah kicked him right in the stomach and he dropped.

"Now," Jonah said, staring down on him, "you can either leave while you're still breathing, or stay and don't."

He collected himself and stood in front of us, an egg-sized bulb on the side of his face. "This is not over." His stare landed right on me. "For anyone." He turned to go, slamming the door behind him.

I rushed to Carmen and held her tightly; her blue eyes had a sea of water in them. "Are you okay?" I examined her. "I'm so sorry, C."

She replied between sobs, "I wasn't...gonna let him...hurt you. Not...again." She held me tighter with each word.

I smiled empathetically, knowing my best friend put herself before me. After a while, I let go and turned towards Jonah, who was rubbing his fire-colored fist. Blood dripped from his nose.

I cautiously stepped closer to him and said, "You didn't have to do that."

"You're right," he said. "But I wanted to."

I hugged him tighter than I had ever hugged anyone in my life. "Thank you," I whispered.

"Hope." Carmen touched my shoulder. "I think you should go with Jonah. You will feel more safe."

"No," Jonah refused, "she needs her best friend. You can have my ticket."

"I have an idea." I looked at both of them. "What if we all go? C, I have some money saved up from working at the bar, and I know you've been saving for a car but—"

"It sounds perfect." Carmen smiled. "I think we should get Astrid in on this, too. You know, considering she's practically a native there."

"The flight leaves tomorrow night," said Jonah. "So we better get packing. I have to go. But I'll come pick you guys up around four." Only then did I realize we were still holding hands when he let go.

"Goodbye," I whispered long after he was gone.

Carmen grinned at me mischievously.

"What?" I said too defensively.

"Don't 'what' me. You were in a *closet. Naked.*"

"Nothing happened. Listen, I'm gonna go to bed, but there's something I have to do first."

I jumped into bed, pulled out my phone and sent one last text. *I can't do this anymore. I'm done.*

Send. I shut my eyes, and replayed the day in my head. I never had felt more content and scared, but I was excited for what tomorrow would bring.

FIVE

2:42PM. ASTRID HAD JUST ARRIVED AT OUR DORM as Carmen and I scrambled to pack our things.

"Would this shirt make me look good?" Carmen asked as she twirled around, admiring herself in the mirror.

"You obviously know it makes you look good," I chuckled as I threw a hoodie at her.

Astrid coughed and added, "It's Cleveland Penitentiary, C. Not New York Fashion Week."

Something was bubbling up inside of me, and it wasn't alcohol. It was excitement. Anxiousness. Relief. Stress. All jumbled up into one body.

"I hope he will even want to see me," I said. "He hasn't written back in like four months."

"Maybe he was busy?" Carmen suggested.

"Yeah, life in prison can be a real handful." Astrid rolled her eyes.

I shrugged and continued packing when my phone vibrated. *9 missed calls, 27 unread messages.* I paused for a moment before hitting the "Block This Number" button. But as soon as I did, I felt a wave of relief rush over me.

3:51pm. Jonah would be here any minute.

"I'm gonna go freshen up before we head to the airport," I told my friends.

My cheek was starting to turn an ugly blue-brown color, and my knee was wrapped up with gauze. I spent some time working on my hair, more than I had in a while. I threw on some powder and mascara, more makeup than I had worn in weeks. I changed out of my three-year-old Tampa Bay shirt and into a soft blue tee. I took a spritz of Carmen's perfume and a swipe of her lip gloss.

"Damn," Astrid teased as I walked back into the bedroom. "Since when does Hope touch her hair?"

"And her face," Carmen added suspiciously, examining me up and down. She smelled my neck. "Pretty sure that's *my* perfume and lip gloss that you're wearing," she said with a wink.

Two knocks hit the door and Astrid went to answer it. "Hey, Jonah."

"You guys ready?" he asked.

"More than ever," replied Carmen.

"Absolutely," said Astrid.

I nodded and forced a smile.

Jonah gave me a confused look but continued, "All right, ladies! Our trip to Ohio officially starts now."

We piled into the taxi waiting outside for us and sped towards the airport. Our flight was in an hour and thirteen minutes.

"So that gives us exactly twenty-one minutes to get there, thirteen minutes to check in, fifteen minutes to go through security, and fourteen minutes to loiter," Astrid calculated. "The flight from Tampa to Cleveland is about two-and-a-half hours, so I hope you guys brought your homework."

"Thanks for the math lesson," Jonah mocked. He looked at me and asked, "Are you nervous?"

"Terrified," I answered.

His hand lightly squeezed my thigh and he said, "We're all going to be right there with you. There's no need to worry."

I half-smiled and turned my attention to the road. We were in standstill traffic.

"Hope," Astrid turned to me, "I really need to tell you some—"

"Um, excuse me." Carmen tapped on the driver's shoulder. "Isn't there an exit you can take or something to get out of this mess?"

"No," replied the man with a heavy accent. "No exit for fourteen miles."

"Fourteen?" said the choir of passengers.

5:21. Our plane was supposed to leave at 6:30.

"Traffic will take while," said the driver.

"Shit." Jonah pressed his hand to his head.

"How far away from the airport are we, sir?" I prompted.

"Fifteen minutes. Forty-five in traffic."

I swung open the yellow door. "Let's go," I ordered.

"What?" Carmen exclaimed. "We're in the middle of a highway!"

"No way," said Astrid. "All that carbon dioxide is not healthy for the lungs."

Jonah followed me out the car and grabbed our luggage. "Well, I guess we'll just meet you there then?"

"Ugh!" pouted Carmen as she slid out the vehicle. "I'm coming."

"Astrid?" I coaxed.

The poor girl looked petrified, like she was about to go on a death mission.

"C'mon, I'll be right next to you," I said as I reached out my arm.

A shaky hand grabbed mine and was pulled out of the taxi, all four of us in the breakdown lane with our luggage.

"This is insane," Carmen commented.

"I like insane." Jonah smiled.

Carmen pretended to gag and rolled her eyes to the sky. 5:34pm.

"We have no time to waste." I sounded like a general directing my soldiers. "We have less than an hour to get on that plane. Astrid, how much time does that give us?"

She coughed and replied, "Well, it will take approximately thirty-nine minutes to walk there if we are quick, and that leaves us..." She thought for a second. "...eight minutes for check-in, nine minutes for security." The color drained from her face.

We were in a single file line, the cold air blowing on my face and the sun starting to fall beneath the clouds. The highway looked like a parking lot, and by now our taxi looked like a toy car from where we were.

6:11. We were two minutes ahead of schedule. We were all quite relieved to see the airport; our legs were exhausted. Astrid was in the front with the tickets, followed by Carmen, Jonah, and me trailing behind.

"H! Let's go!" Carmen called from ahead.

I was standing in front of the doors, staring at the airport.

"We have exactly nineteen minutes!" Astrid tapped her phone.

My breathing started to quicken. My hands began to shake. "I can't," I whispered.

Jonah turned around and ran up to me, his big hands rubbing my arms, "Hey, hey, hey," he cooed. "You're gonna be okay."

I turned my head away. I kept telling myself not to cry, begging myself to stay strong.

He turned my chin so we were face to face. "You need to talk to me. You can trust me. You trust me, right, H?"

I was silent.

"Oh," he said as he backed away. "I see." Astrid tried to grab his arm but he stormed off.

"We don't have time to stage a soap opera!" Carmen took my hand and dragged me to security. The three of us took off our shoes and walked through the body scanners.

"What was that all about?" Astrid questioned as she put her dirty high-tops back on.

I shook my head and slipped on my moccasins. "I'm sure he's at the terminal. I just don't feel like sitting next to him on that plane."

Carmen zipped up her booties. "We have eight minutes. Let's go."

We rushed to section C just as the first class passengers began to board.

"I don't see him," said Astrid as her pupils darted back and forth.

"I'll go find him." I dropped my bags and ran about the airport.

6:25 pm. I called his phone, but no answer.

6:31pm. He wasn't at any of the restaurants or shops.

6:36pm. He wasn't outside.

I sprinted back to the terminal. 6:40pm.

"Last call for flight 3B to Cleveland, last call for flight 3B to Cleveland." called a miserable voice over the intercom.

The last group of passengers was boarding as I ran up to the flight attendant's desk, feeling winded and defeated.

"Okay, miss," said a way too perky employee as she handed me back my ticket. "You are going to be sitting in row F, seat three. I believe your friends left you these bags."

"Thanks," I mumbled. Tears welled up in my eyes knowing that Jonah was gone. I turned to take one last look at the airport, grabbed my belongings, and boarded the plane.

SIX

MY HEAD HUNG AS THE FLIGHT ATTENDANT WEL-
comed me aboard. I slid into my seat next to the
window, the only one in my row. Carmen and Astrid
were a few aisles up, laughing away. I gazed out the
window, ready for the plane to take off. The sky was
black now, and the first stars were appearing. Everyone was quiet; there was some sort of tension mixed
in the air of the plane. The lights were obnoxiously
bright. I pulled out the current book I was reading
and shoved in my earbuds, but I was completely out
of focus. I sighed, slammed my book shut and turned
up my music. A few moments later, a tap on my
shoulder startled me.

"Hey," Jonah said, and he sat down in the seat
next to me.

I was floored. "Wait, how did—"

"I was just in the bathroom. When I stormed off like an idiot I just went on the plane. I was one of the first people to board," he explained. "I'm really sorry for causing a scene like that."

"No, I'm sorry. I *do* trust you, I was just really nervous to get on this plane. I guess the closer I get to my father, the more anxious I get."

He placed his hand in mine. "You're going to be fine, Hope. I'm gonna be right there with you, for everything." His hazel eyes met my deep brown ones and lingered there for what seemed like a century. He leaned closer to me.

"Alright passengers, flight 3B to Cleveland is about to begin. Prepare for takeoff."

"Sorry," I said, after the pilot finished speaking. "What were you saying?"

"Yeah, um. I—"

"Would you two like any peanuts or beverages?"

"No," I answered the attendant, more rudely than I intended.

Jonah rolled his eyes. "Never mind."

I chuckled, leaned my head on his shoulder and sighed a breath of relief.

"I'm really glad you're here," I said as I nuzzled into his chest.

He spoke softly. "Me too." His arm wrapped around me and he planted a kiss on my forehead.

I felt the beating of his heart, I heard the soft

engine of the plane, and peered out the window. The stars were just starting to appear in the sky, each one shining with its own purpose. I could hear the laughs of the other passengers and saw the dimming of the plane lights as one by one, patrons began to fall asleep. I closed my eyes, and for once in my life, I felt peace rush through my whole body.

SEVEN

I WOKE UP TO A RINGING IN MY EARS AND A SNOR-ing Jonah beside me.

"Welcome to Cleveland, folks. It is currently nine-sixteen pm, dark and chilly. Thank you for a great flight, and we hope you'll join us again."

I grabbed a piece of gum and smacked it until my ears popped. I awkwardly shook Jonah awake.

"Good morning," he said groggily with one eye open.

"Not really," I giggled. "It's almost nine-thirty. We just landed."

Just then the lights came back on. A chorus of passengers moaned and began to collect their belongings.

"Let's go find Carmen and Astrid." I stood up and grabbed my carry-on.

He did the same, and we exited the plane. We

joined the girls, who were stretching and looked tired as ever.

"Hey, you two," Carmen said with a yawn. "Pretty good flight."

"Welcome to Cleveland," said Astrid. "My grandma has a car waiting for us outside."

"A car?" I asked.

"Well, yeah," she replied bashfully. "*Halmeoni* has been pretty successful since she brought rare goods here from Korea."

We all eyed each other and shrugged. After going to baggage claim, we walked outside to a cold Cleveland night with a man in a suit holding a sign that read "Yin" in big letters. The four of us piled into a stretch limo, equipped with leather seats and a wine fridge. I reached for a bottle and Carmen slapped my hand.

"What?" I asked.

She just shot me a glare and sipped her champagne innocently.

"Drink?" She offered Astrid, as if it was her vehicle.

"No, no." She shot her down quickly. "I can't."

Carmen gave her a confused look and scrolled through her phone.

The drive was long, and by the time we arrived at her house, Carmen had her head on my shoulder and I was in the middle of a dream.

"Welcome to Namja Mansion," the driver told us as we pulled into a long circular driveway, complete with a stone fountain and well-trimmed bushes.

"Whoa." Jonah gaped as he got out of the limo.

Astrid smiled nervously and changed the subject. "Let's go inside, I'm wiped out."

We followed her up a brick staircase to two over-sized doors. They opened to a very grand entrance with espresso floors, a crystal chandelier, and white trim. A mix of classic and contemporary Asian art hung on the walls, and modern furniture consumed the many rooms.

"I could get used to this." Carmen was smiling ear-to-ear as she waltzed around the room.

"This is incredible," Jonah awed as his head moved in every direction.

My mouth dropped as I took everything in. A staircase with a cast-iron railing spun up the thirteen-foot ceilings above me, and I felt a soft fur rug in between my toes below me. I could smell lavender and other oils. I felt so out of place in such an upper-class environment.

Astrid shouted something in Korean before saying, "Take off your shoes. It's a sign of respect."

We followed her order just as an old woman hobbled down the stairs in a silk robe, her grey hair pulled back in a low knot.

"Welcome, welcome!" she said in an accent thicker than her granddaughter's. "I am Yeon, but call me *Halmeoni.*"

We exchanged names and she hugged us all. "I am so happy Astrid brought friends," she said with a smile. "This house can get lonely."

She led each of us to our rooms, which were no less extravagant than downstairs. They were all located in one wing and were stocked with huge, white beds, a gorgeous view of the city, and televisions that probably cost more than my college tuition.

"If you need me," Yeon said, "I'll be three doors down to the left."

We all settled in quite nicely; I had just gotten into bed when I heard a knock at my door.

"H?" someone whispered.

It was Carmen in a pink nightie, her hair in a perfect bun. "Can I stay with you tonight?"

"Please," I answered.

She climbed into the king-sized bed and forced a smile. "It's different here, but I like it."

"It's amazing," I replied quietly.

"I think I'm just as nervous as you are for tomorrow. What are you even gonna say? 'Hi, we haven't talked in almost half a year but I'm being abused by my ex-boyfriend?'"

"I didn't really plan it all out. I wouldn't even know where to begin."

"Well, you better figure it out soon, honey. It's only ten hours away."

I shook my head and turned to my side, but

Carmen said one last thing.

"Hey, I'm proud of you," and she turned to face the door.

I hugged my teddy bear to my chest, fell asleep easily, and was taken back to my childhood.

There were bangs at the door that sounded like a snare drum. Mom opened it and pointed to her room as three men in blue uniforms tore up the house.

"Mommy, what's happening?" I asked, gripping onto my teddy bear for dear life.

"No, sweetie, go back to your room. Mommy has to handle something," she answered frantically.

"Are they taking Daddy?" I asked, tears dripping down my tiny cheeks.

Just then, the three men stormed out of Mom's room with Dad in cuffs, his hands held over his head.

"Just let me say goodbye to my kid," he begged. "Please!"

"You have the right to remain silent," one of them said, and pulled out a baton which he slapped him in the gut with.

"Daddy!" I cried and ran towards him, but Mom gripped me tight in her arms.

"No!" I wailed. "Don't take my dad!"

Mom was trying to hold me back, but my infant self was no match for her. I hugged his leg tight and sobbed, "Daddy, don't leave me!"

"I'm sorry, baby," he said as the officer hit him again.

"Don't hit him! No!" I yelled at the tall man. He yanked me off my father and I slid across the linoleum floor.

The men rushed the culprit out of the house.

"Daddy! Daddy!" I was hysterical, running after them but the front door slammed in my face. I was blinded by tears. I fell to my knees and cried, "Daddy! Daddy! Daddy!"

I sat up, gasping for air, sweat dripping from my forehead. I looked wildly around the room as my eyes adjusted to my surroundings. 2:56am. I took a deep breath and tiptoed out of the room, careful not to disturb Carmen.

I quietly shut the door and trudged down the hall, looking for the nearest bathroom, when an unpleasant sound filled my ears. I followed the noise to Astrid's bathroom, with her on her knees, vomiting over the toilet.

My hand covered my mouth. My body went numb. I ran to Yeon's room in search of help.

EIGHT

"YEON!" I WHISPER-SHOUTED AND SWUNG HER door open.

"Yes? Yes?" She shot up and felt for her glasses. "What is it, *kkul?*"

"Astrid," I sputtered, out of breath, "She's...she's sick."

Yeon nodded softly as if she was used to this.

"I know what to do," she said as she got out of bed.

The ambulance came within minutes; all of us stood in the driveway in our pajamas. Carmen was crying into Jonah's chest, and I turned to Yeon.

"What's happening?" I asked through sniffles.

"This is normal." She shook her head in despair. When I returned with a perplexed stare, she rolled her eyes.

"What did she tell you of her life back home?" Yeon whispered.

"Um..." I racked my brain "That she moved here with you because her parents died in a car crash. That must have been so hard for her."

"*Gidae*," she said softly, "Astrid didn't tell you the real story."

"What's the real story?" I pressed.

"I will tell you when we get there." She turned to the group of young adults. "We need to go. *Now*."

She waved to the driver and we sped to the emergency room. When we arrived, Yeon rushed out of the car and ran straight to Astrid's room; no other visitors were allowed.

We all sat in a dirty waiting room, which was oddly quiet except for a woman with tissues in her hand and an obnoxious ticking.

The three of us held hands and hung our heads.

"Yeon said Astrid has been lying to us," I spoke abruptly.

"About what?" Carmen questioned.

"Her life at home," I replied. "I think it has something to do with why we're here."

We sat there in silence for over an hour until Yeon appeared, her eyes bloodshot.

"Visitors are welcome," she said. "Doctor said that she will not be awake for a long time."

"What do you mean by 'long time?'" Carmen shot

up out of the filthy chair.

Yeon rushed out of the waiting room, unable to hold back her tsunami of tears.

Without communication, we all ran into the hospital room to find Astrid in a white bed with tubes running up her nose, through her arms, throat, all connected to a sizable machine that displayed her fast-beating heart.

For a moment, we all stood there, speechless. A nurse walked in and gave us the status of her situation: she was suffering from an unknown foreign disease, one which leads to severe swelling of the lungs and throat, constant coughing, and projectile vomiting. She said that they rushed her onto life support after she became unconscious in the ambulance. She hasn't woken up since. Carmen hugged herself and began to sob hysterically, and I turned into Jonah as silent tears fell on his shirt.

"I can't do this," I whispered, and I sprinted out of the room as fast as I could. I ran down the endless hallway; I could feel my heart thumping in my ears and throat. My eyes were blinded by tears as I tried to dodge other doctors and visitors in the corridor.

I slammed the door open and felt the cold air blast my face. I shivered, gasped for a breath, and stared into the dark night as I screamed in frustration. How could something so awful happen to such an amazing person?

I felt a cold hand on my shoulder followed by a warm blanket put around me. I turned to find Yeon, who looked as sad as ever. She sat down on the curb and I joined her.

"Is she going to be okay?" I asked, staring at the street, already knowing the answer.

"I don't know, *Gidae.* But for now, that's all we can do."

My eyes met hers. "Can you finish telling me her real story?"

She sighed as a single tear escaped her brown orbs.

NINE

"ASTRID WAS BORN A HAPPY BABY," SHE BEGAN.
"Her mother was an alcoholic, so she came out a tiny one. Doctors said she would not grow to be over five feet, a birth defect from all of the wine. Her name means 'Godly strength,' and she certainly lived up to it.

"Her *abejoi* was a big man in Korea; he was head of a company that made parts for many cars. When Astrid was just four years old, he sent her to work in the factory. Her father was a mean man. He used to hit her if she did not get the job done. If anyone tried to stop him, they would just suffer his wrath, too.

"Astrid caught a rare disease from the factory fumes. Doctors there tried to heal her, but the old technology there was of no help. She would often cough blood and would get sick once a week.

"Her mother was no different. She would get drunk and abuse her if Astrid didn't complete her chores. I remember her knocking on my door, late at night, begging me to let her sleep in my home. Her face would always be bruised; her little fingers bloody and weak from working so much.

"Eventually Astrid became a resident at my house, and her parents didn't like it. They would show up at my door and try to take her home, and when I refused, they would beat me.

"I couldn't take it anymore. The fighting, the beating, the constant feeling of living in fear. So I did the most risky thing I possibly could: I packed my things, cut off ties completely with her parents, took Astrid, and moved to America with the little money I had."

We both tried not to cry as she continued. "The first few years were hard. Many birthdays went without gifts, many Christmases without trees. Luckily, I had some rare goods shipped here from home and made a small fortune selling them.

"Her parents tried to contact both of us, but after her father's business failed, there was no way they could afford a flight here. So we are safe for now.

"Astrid's cough was minimal when we started our new life here. She just began to relapse this year." Yeon shook her head. "I never imagined in all of my years that it would get this bad."

Yeon lost it. She started to bawl uncontrollably,

her whole body shaking. "I just don't want her to go before I do," she managed to get out.

I hugged her tightly. "If there's one thing I know about Astrid, it's that she's a fighter. She will get through this," I told her. "I know it."

Yeon forced a smile and mouthed the words, "thank you." I nodded and stood up.

"C'mon." I reached out my hand. "Let's go keep her company. I'm sure she needs her *Halmeoni* right now."

She chuckled. "Your Korean is getting better," she said, and took my hand.

We walked back into the room to see Jonah and Carmen kneeling by Astrid, his arm around her.

"How is she?" I whispered.

Carmen shook her head and shrugged in defeat.

Jonah opened his other arm to me and I rested my head on his shoulder. The three of us appreciated each other's company, each other's warmth, as we all gazed upon our friend. Jonah carefully rested his hand on hers, Carmen followed, and I did the same.

A wrinkly hand was placed on top of mine. Yeon smiled at all of us.

"Keep this friendship," she said. "You all need each other. Don't take it for granted. Because you never know..." her attention turned to Astrid, "...when it is going to be your time."

TEN

I WOKE UP IN THE SAME GRIMY WAITING ROOM. I
opened my eyes gradually and turned to the right to
see my hand interlocked with Carmen's. I turned to
my left to see my other hand in Jonah's, all of us sitting in old, black chairs. A large grey blanket covered
our legs.

I nudged both of them; they moaned, groaned,
and stretched almost simultaneously. Carmen had
one eye open and turned on her phone.

"It's six thirty-seven." She yawned.

"We're supposed to go see my dad in an hour and
a half." I stood up, but looked thoughtfully back at
the hallway that led to Astrid's room.

"Let's go see if she's okay," Jonah suggested.

When we arrived, Yeon had her hand in Astrid's,
her head hung low, yet she was still wide awake.

"How is she?" Carmen cautiously stepped towards the patient.

"Doctors are delving more into their research," Yeon said. "She lost a lot of blood when she was vomiting."

Astrid's heart was beating rapidly and her fingers would often squirm.

"Let's stay here today," I said. "She needs us."

Yeon stood and looked up at me. "Astrid would have wanted you to go."

"I'll stay here," Carmen offered as she touched my shoulder. "If you're okay with that. Jonah will be there with you, plus Yeon could use some company."

Yeon and Carmen exchanged smiles.

My heart was going almost as fast as Astrid's as I considered my options.

"It's what you came here for," Jonah said softly.

"Let's do it." I managed a smile and looked at Jonah; our stare connected for a few seconds.

"We'll be back as soon as we can," Jonah said. He took my hand and we ran down the hallway, which seemed even longer than before. We each slammed open a door to a dark morning. Grey clouds spat out tiny raindrops, and the black tar started to fill with puddles. The sun was trying to peek through but continually got eaten up by a rush of overcast. Yeon's driver was still there, so we hopped into the car.

"Cleveland Penitentiary," I said to the driver, my

hand grasping Jonah's for dear life. I peered out the window, viewing the trees, the street signs, the pedestrians, all intermixed into a sea of colors. Raindrops raced across the window, each of different sizes. I watched them as they slammed against the window guards, disappearing.

The driver pulled up to a dark mahogany-colored building that stretched to the sky. Rain seeped through the wires of the ominous grey fence that surrounded the place.

I dodged puddles as I slowly walked towards the glass-paned doors. My head spun in every direction, memories flooding back to me, one wave at a time until they crashed inside the edges of my brain.

I halted, looking up at the huge structure in front of me. It was laughing at me, mocking me. I felt like I was six years old again, or at least I felt that small.

Mom pulled me out of the taxi and she held my hand as we walked down a long pathway that led to elaborate glass doors.

"Mommy, where are we?" I asked.

"This is where Daddy will be for a long time," Mom replied.

"Why? When's he coming home?" I said nervously.

"I don't know, Hopie."

"Why?"

Suddenly a black car came to an abrupt stop in front of the penitentiary. The same three men got out of the vehicle, forming a triangle around a man in handcuffs.

The men were like soldiers, marching in perfect rhythm. I watched in awe as the men stomped closer to me, and realized the man that was surrounded by the officers was my father.

"Daddy!" *I cried.*

He turned his head towards me, his right cheek swollen and an ugly red color. For once, I saw the same pain in his eyes that I had seen in my mother's for so many years.

"Hope?" Jonah brought me back to reality and I jumped a little.

"I can't, Jonah." I shook my head in despair. "I just can't do it. It's bringing back too many memories."

"You can't be scared," Jonah comforted me. "You have to be brave."

"I can't be brave!" I yelled. "I can't. I can't, I can't, I can't." I began to shake.

"Hope—"

"What?!"

His lips pressed against mine as his warm hands cupped my face. My eyes widened to the sizes of saucers, but my lids closed ever so softly. We both held on for far too long; I twisted the back of his blonde hair between my fingers, and his hands grazed along my torso until they landed firmly upon my waist and hugged my sides.

His bright hazel eyes were smiling as he was against the wall. He reached to hold my hand but his fingers were covered in mud from the siding of the building. We laughed for a moment at his clumsiness and walked inside. We told the less-than-friendly receptionist who we were going to see, and we were led to a dark room by a man in blue.

"You have ten minutes," he grumbled as he trudged away.

The room was dimly lit by fluorescent lighting from about two decades ago. There was a table that connected to a clear Plexiglas wall that went from the floor to ceiling. I sat on one of the rusted, silver stools and peered inside. Each side had black bars that stretched as far as I could see. The hallway was mostly empty, except for a few guards who stood stagnant. There were so many people locked up, but it seemed so lifeless. One of the men with a black baton moved towards a cell in the far right corner and turned a key into the lock. The bars swung open slowly and creaked.

Two tattered black boots plodded down the hall-way in their own rhythm, the sound filling up the whole room. *Stomp...stomp...stomp.* His legs were covered in faded orange cloth that followed up his torso, chest, and arms, showcasing his huge muscles. His face was surrounded by scruff and his bald head reflected the dated lighting.

His brown eyes, which looked exactly like mine, were screaming in shock. "Hi, Hope," said my father.

ELEVEN

A SHAKY BREATH ESCAPED MY MOUTH. JONAH rubbed my thigh in a comforting manner. We quickly exchanged looks and I turned back to him.

"H-hi," I sputtered. We could actually feel the tension in the air.

"How are you, dear?" he questioned, his breath becoming visible on the Plexiglas.

I didn't know how to answer, where to begin. My mind had a million things to say, but my lips were mute. I frantically searched for something to say, anything.

"Actually, she's not good," Jonah replied for me. I sighed a breath of relief and continued for him.

"Dad," I began. "How did you feel when you hurt Mom?"

He was completely taken back. The only sound in the room was our uneven breaths. I could see his brain flipping upside down.

"Well, at first, I felt empowered," he said softly. "But then I felt an indescribable feeling. A feeling that made my heart drop into my stomach." He sniffled, but then coughed it away. "Because then I realized, when someone becomes so hurt, they hurt the people they love."

"Why didn't you stop?" I asked.

"It was like a disease. Once I started I couldn't stop. It was an escape, a cruel, awful escape. The pain I saw in her eyes only made me want to hurt her more. I figured if I kept hurting her I wouldn't have to see him."

He shook his head in frustration and disappointment. But his brown eyes reflected in mine and this time he asked me a question.

"Hope, why did you come here?" he said.

I stood up off the stool. I pulled up my sleeve to show the bruises on my wrists. I took my phone out to show him the pictures of my cheek and my leg.

I watched the oxygen escape from his body. His placed his calloused hand on the glass that divided us, and I did the same. A tear rolled quickly down his cheek.

The officer came and tried to take Dad away, but he resisted.

"Let's go," said the man sternly, his hand placed over his back pocket.

"Just let me say goodbye to my kid," he begged.

"Just let me say goodbye to my kid," he begged. "Please!"

"Please!"

"Daddy!" I cried.

"Dad!" I cried. I tried to reach forward but Jonah restrained me.

Mom held me back, tight in her arms.

"Let's go!" yelled the officer, and hit him.

The officer slapped him with his baton.

"No! Don't touch my father!"

"Don't hit my daddy!"

"I'm sorry, baby."

"I'm sorry, baby."

As the men dragged him away, he whipped his head around and shouted, "He's not a man if he touches you, Hope. He's not a man!"

They slammed the cell shut.

They slammed the door shut in my face.

I fell to my knees. I felt the walls closing in on me. I shook my head violently. I keeled over and gasped for what little air was in the room. My insides were caving, my brain was shrinking and then grew, shrank and grew. Inhale, exhale. Inhale, exhale. Inhale, inhale, inhale, inhale...

Jonah embraced my whole body, he leaned his head on top of mine and pulled me tight into his chest, our breaths going together in perfect time. I held him close, my shaking subsiding, my head clearing, my heart rate slowing down. I sighed, and counted my blessings.

TWELVE

JONAH TOOK MY HAND AND WE HEADED OUT OF THE penitentiary. Surprisingly, our spirits were high. We exited the doors and walked into a sunny afternoon. The rain was drying up from the ground and the dark, ominous clouds had turned into light, fluffy ones. It was warmer than usual and everyone around us seemed to be in a good mood.

We slowly strolled down the path and turned the corner to catch a cab. I was looking up to Jonah with bright eyes, lusting over everything about him.

I halted in the middle of the sidewalk. My whole body turned to ice. I could feel a familiar feeling on the back of my neck. I slowly twisted my head, and the last thing I remember is hearing screams all around me, falling onto concrete and the world going black.

THIRTEEN

FROM JONAH'S PERSPECTIVE

I SPUN AROUND TO SEE HOPE FACE DOWN ON THE sidewalk, and him rubbing his blistering knuckles. Our stares met. I jumped to her side, shaking her, checking for a pulse or any sign of life. Her heart was beating rapidly.

I stood up slowly, my eyes closing in on him. I rushed up to him and grabbed him by the collar of his shirt. I was taller than him, stronger than him. I threw him against the brick wall, my hands turning red from my grip.

"How could you do this to her?" I shrieked. "How—what—why are you here? You don't belong here! Look at what you're doing to her!" I couldn't even keep track of what I was saying.

"Hey man, just let go of me," he said frantically. The menace in his eyes turned into fear.

I slammed his back against the wall again.

"You're weak," I sneered. "You're a coward. You're in so much pain that you're hurting the ones you love." My heavy breath was blowing his black hair out of his face.

"Let go of me."

"You don't even realize how much pain she is in."

"Let *go* of me."

"You're *abusing* her!"

"*Let go of me!*"

I flung his shirt out of my hands and backed away. As I turned my attention to Hope, he grabbed my shoulder forcefully.

"Just let me know if she's—"

With all of my might, I swung a punch to his right cheek. He dropped immediately and stayed there.

"You stay the hell away from her," I pointed to him, and watched him carry himself away.

"Hope," I whispered in her ear, "it's me. God, please wake up. Please wake up."

Tears were welling up in my eyes. I tried to hold myself together.

"Please wake up, Hope. Please, please, please."

I placed a soft kiss on her lips, pulled out my phone and called for help. I rubbed her ice cold hand and waited for the ambulance to come.

"I love you," I breathed.

FOURTEEN

FROM JONAH'S PERSPECTIVE

THE EMTS LIFTED HER TO A GURNEY AND CAREFULLY
placed her in the ambulance. I rode by her side the
whole way there, refusing to let go of her hand.
The doctors had her hooked up to a monitor with
clear tubes running up her nose. When we arrived,
Carmen was in the waiting room with Yeon. They
both jumped out of their chairs as the EMTs jogged
her to the nearest room.

"What is happening?" Yeon exclaimed as she ran
by the gurney's side.

"Oh no, not again. Not again," Carmen cried, running by the other.

They lay her on the bed and shoved a needle in
her wrist.

"Make sure she's okay," I mentioned and received
glares by the nurses in return.

I sat by her side looking over her, talking to her, telling her all of the things I was afraid to say if she was awake.

A man with grey scruff and thinning hair walked into the room. He pulled his glasses out of his white coat and started scribbling on a clipboard.

"Okay," he said with a sigh. "How did this happen?" he asked, never looking up from his paper. As if he'd asked the same question a hundred times.

I fumbled with my words as I explained to the miserable doctor what had happened. He lowered his clipboard and yanked his glasses off. He sat down next to me and asked for the information of the man who had assaulted Hope. I turned to Hope and reluctantly gave the doctor his name and contact information.

"Thank you," he said as he wrote it all down. The doctor looked back up at me and said, "You must really care for her, huh?"

"Yeah." I paused. "I do."

After a few minutes of inspection, he told me that she had been mildly concussed, but it was not too serious. He also said she had fractured a small bone in her nose that could be healed in a few weeks with some gauze. There was some bruising underneath her eyes and a good-sized red egg on her forehead. He asked if there was a parent or a guardian around, so I brought in Yeon, with Carmen close at her heels. He handed her the proper medication that she needed and informed us he had to contact the police by law.

Yeon left to go attend to Astrid, who was still asleep. Carmen followed soon after, and I was the only one left with her.

I pulled my chair right up to her bedside and admired her, even when she was asleep.

"Um, hi," I began awkwardly. "So, I really, really like you, Hope. You're so strong, even if you don't realize it. You're one of the strongest people I know, actually. I just wish you knew exactly how I felt. I care about you so much, Hope. I pray to God that one day I'm able to call you mine."

I sat there in silence for a few moments, looking out the window to the buildings being coated with drops of rain and the trees in a brawl with the wind. The clouds were starting to spread out, the sun just barely peeking through.

Her fingers twitched. I whipped around and saw her eyes stirring, her hand lightly squeezing my own. She half-opened her gorgeous brown eyes and accustomed herself to her surroundings.

"Hi, Jonah," she whispered. Her head turned to mine and she gave me a small grin.

"Hey," I cooed. "How are you feeling? Do you need anything? I mean Carmen is out there. I can—"

"Just shut up," she giggled and pulled my face to hers, her soft lips lightly pressing onto mine.

"I heard everything you said," she told me sheepishly. "Was all of that really true?"

I blushed.

"Every word," I replied, our lips centimeters apart. "You're perfect, Hope. You make me so happy." I placed a kiss on her nose and stared into her glistening eyes.

"And him?" she wiped a tear.

"The authorities said they'd find him within twenty-four hours. He's not going anywhere near you, I promise. You're safe."

"You make me feel safe," she said, and sighed as she nestled into my chest.

I planted my lips on her forehead and closed my eyes, soaking in the warmth of her skin and listening to the beating of her heart.

FIFTEEN

FROM HOPE'S PERSPECTIVE

AFTER A DAY OR TWO I WAS RESTLESS TO ESCAPE from this room with beige walls that smelled like detergent. A few nurses stood uneasily by my bed as I got up.

"I'm fine," I snapped, refusing to accept help from any of them.

I slowly walked to the bathroom, my muscles weak and my head in pain. I grabbed the wall and leaned against it.

Inhale, exhale. Inhale, exhale.

The hallway suddenly turned into my school corridor.

The next thing I knew, I was being dragged into the girl's lavatory. Two big hands had my wrists pinned against the wall and a pair of feet crushed my tiny toes.

I sank to the floor.

"You think you can just ignore me, bitch? Huh?" His breath tickled my neck and went right down my spine as I started to scream. His hand slammed against my face and I keeled over in pain, unable to get any noise or word out. His arms had my wrists so tight in his hands that they began to bruise.

"No, no, no," I repeated, shaking my head violently. My hands covered my face.

"Answer my goddamn question. I'm not gonna ask you again." He kicked my leg and raised his fist for a second time.

"No, no, no, I'm sorry! I'm sorry," I wailed out loud. "I'm sorry."

I was gripping my blue gown tight, tears flooding my face.

"I'm okay," I told no one. "I'm okay. I'm going to be okay."

I hesitated, knowing the last five words that came out of my mouth were not true.

"You're not okay," I conversed with myself. "You're weak. You're not okay."

A body slid across the floor to embrace mine.

"Shhh. You're okay. You're safe. I promise."

Carmen managed a smile. "You're okay."

I cried into her shoulder. I cried because I was sad. I cried because I was scared. I cried because I was relieved. There was no more fighting, no more hurt, no more pain. I felt free. I felt terrified. I didn't really know what I was feeling. All I knew was that I had survived.

ƐPILOGUE

15 MONTHS LATER

"HOW WAS IT?"

"Good," I said, shutting the car door and fastening my seatbelt.

Jonah fiddled with the wheel.

"Was it weird, you know, considering it was your last day?"

"I guess so," I replied. "I actually kind of enjoyed therapy."

"Are you ready to go back to the dorm? The Graduation Ball is in like three hours."

"Let's go." I shared a quick kiss with him and turned my attention to the window. The sun was just beginning to set and the trees were blossoming with beautiful pastel colors. The few white clouds smiled down upon me, the birds smiled down upon me, Mom smiled down upon me, telling me they were proud of me. I fumbled my necklace between my fingers and leaned my head on the car door.

"Wow," I said.

"Yeah, wow."

Carmen and I were both staring in the mirror, her in a short dress that complemented her blue eyes and me in a red dress that stretched to the floor.

"You look amazing," we both said simultaneously, and burst into giggles.

"If Jonah doesn't faint when he sees you tonight, I don't know what I'm going to do with myself." Carmen fixed my curled brown hair so it fell perfectly across my face and touched up my eyeliner that took her practically a century to do.

"There." She stepped back proudly. "Perfect."

She rubbed my shoulders as we both looked at my reflection.

"I'm so proud of you," she told me.

"It's gonna be weird leaving this place in a few weeks." I gazed around our room which was surrounded by boxes and piles of junk.

Carmen ran away into the closet. She reappeared, covered in a tattered pink towel.

"Oh, Jonah!" she moaned teasingly. "It's so dark in this closet."

"Shut up." I laughed nostalgically.

I picked up my dress and walked down the grand staircase that spun to a dance floor complete with about three hundred of my classmates, who all whipped their heads around to catch a glimpse of the new me. Out of all of them, my eyes drew to the man in the grey suit with dirty blonde hair and hazel eyes.

His jaw dropped to his feet as I edged closer to him, my smile radiating.

"Hope—"

My lips glued to his, a soft kiss turning into a strong one. And another one, another one, another one.

I laughed. "Later," I said, and winked. My phone buzzed.

"Yeon? It's so good to hear from you!"

"*Gidae*, it's Astrid."

"Oh no." I grasped Jonah's arm tightly.

"No, it's great news! She woke up from her coma this morning. The doctors said she will be able to return home in less than a month!"

"Oh my God!" Tears welled up in my eyes. "I'm so happy, Yeon. The three of us will be out there as soon as we can to come see her."

"I'm looking forward to it."

I hung up the phone. I told Jonah and Carmen the good news and we planned to book the next flight to Cleveland.

"This is amazing!" Carmen exclaimed.

"What could possibly be better?" I asked.

"I think I know," Jonah smiled as he dropped to his knee.

A year after, Jonah and I said our vows in Cleveland by the water. We continued to stay in touch with Astrid and Carmen, both healthy and happy. Yeon often stopped by our apartment in Tampa for coffee. I occasionally visited my dad, who was soon to be released with parole. My ex was found guilty of severe domestic violence and was sentenced eight to ten years. Sometimes I lay awake at night thinking about him. Others I will dream badly of it and have Jonah hold me until I fall back asleep.

I began advocating for dating violence and raised money for local charities that supported this cause. I learned that violence comes in all different forms. I learned that nearly 20 people are domestically abused per minute by an intimate partner. I learned that sexual abuse is the most common form. I listened to stories of victims and realized how strong we all were.

The most important thing I learned, though, is what real love is.